D0977976

KIDS' SPOR

KEEP DANCING

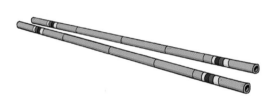

by Cristina Oxtra

illustrated by Seb Burnett

PICTURE WINDOW BOOKS
a capstone imprint

Hillsboro Public Library
Hillsboro, OR
A member of Washington County
COOPERATIVE LIBRARY SERVICES

Kids' Sports Stories is published by Picture Window Books,
an imprint of Capstone.
1710 Roe Crest Drive, North Mankato, Minnesota 56003
www.capstonepub.com

Copyright © 2021 by Capstone. All rights reserved. No part of this
publication may be reproduced in whole or in part, or stored on a
retrieval system, or transmitted in any form or by any means,
electronic, mechanical, photocopying, recording, or otherwise,
without written permission of the publisher.

Library of Congress Cataloging-in-Publication Data
Names: Oxtra, Cristina, author. | Burnett, Seb, illustrator.
Title: Keep dancing / by Cristina Oxtra ; illustrated by Seb Burnett.
Description: North Mankato, Minnesota : Picture Window Books,
an imprint of Capstone, [2021] | Series: Kids' sports stories | Audience:
Ages 5-7. | Audience: Grades K-1. | Summary: Lito and his twin sister,
Nenita, plan to perform a Filipino folk dance at their school's spring
festival, but when snickering classmates threaten to derail
his confidence, Lito learns to dig deep and keep dancing.
Identifiers: LCCN 2020035257 (print) | LCCN 2020035258 (ebook) | ISBN
9781515882442 (hardcover) | ISBN 9781515883531 (paperback) | ISBN
9781515892069 (pdf) | ISBN 9781515892991 (kindle edition)
Subjects: CYAC: Filipino Americans—Fiction. | Folk dancing—Fiction. |
Festivals—Fiction. | Self-confidence—Fiction. | Twins—Fiction. |
Brothers and sisters—Fiction.
Classification: LCC PZ7.1.O895 Ke 2021 (print) | LCC PZ7.1.O895
(ebook) | DDC [E]—dc23
LC record available at https://lccn.loc.gov/2020035257
LC ebook record available at https://lccn.loc.gov/2020035258

Design Elements: Shutterstock: bodrumsurf, 2 (middle bottom);
LN.Vector pattern, 2 (mb); tynyuk, 2, (top)

Designer: Kyle Grenz

33614082268235

Printed and bound in the United States of America.   PO3837

TABLE OF CONTENTS

Glossary

 **athlete**—someone who is well-trained in a sport

 **bamboo**—a hot-weather grass with a hard, hollow stem

 **Philippines**—a country in Southeast Asia; people from there are called Filipinos

 **tinikling** (tee-NEEK-ling)— a dance from the Philippines that features bamboo poles

Chapter 1

YOU DANCE?

Lito and his twin sister, Nenita, were waiting for their dad to pick them up from school. When the car came, Nenita ran toward it.

"Hurry, Lito!" she shouted. "We'll be late for dance class!"

A group of boys heard Nenita.

"You dance?" one of them asked Lito, laughing.

The other boys started laughing too.

"My sister dances," Lito said. "I have to go and watch."

Lito hurried to the car. He got in the back seat with his sister and pulled the door shut.

"I heard what you said to those boys. You lied, Lito," Nenita said, frowning at him. "You dance too."

Lito didn't say anything.

"Why did you lie about dancing?"
Nenita asked. "It's fun, and you're really
good at it."

"I don't want to talk about it," he said.
"You wouldn't understand anyway."

"What's going on back there?" Dad asked.

Before Nenita could answer, Lito said, "Nothing."

He and his sister rode to dance class without another word.

Chapter 2

FALLING DOWN

At class, Lito and Nenita took off their shoes and socks and changed their clothes. They walked onto the dance floor. Two other kids were sitting on the floor, facing each other. Each one held the ends of two long **bamboo** poles.

Lito and Nenita's dance group did dances from the **Philippines**. Lito and Nenita had been practicing the **tinikling**. Soon they were going to perform this special dance at their school's spring festival.

"Ready to dance?" the teacher asked.

"Yes!" the kids yelled—except Lito.

The music started. The two kids with the poles tapped them on the floor twice. Then they clapped the poles together. They did this over and over again.

Tap, tap, clap! Tap, tap, clap!

Lito and Nenita hopped between the moving poles. Tinikling dancers copy the way a tikling bird hops through the grass. As the music speeds up, so do the poles.

Tap, tap, clap! Tap, tap, clap!

Lito was usually quick on his feet. But not today. He tripped and fell to the floor.

"Are you OK, Lito?" the teacher asked.

"I'm fine," Lito said, rubbing his foot.

"I just need to sit down for a minute."

Lito sat down on a bench next to his dad.

"What's wrong, Lito?" Dad asked.

"You're not yourself today."

"I can't dance at the festival, Dad," Lito said. "The boys at school will make fun of me. They play sports. They're **athletes**. I should be an athlete, not a dancer."

"Lito, you work hard on your dancing skills. You are strong and quick," Dad said. "You already *are* an athlete!"

"I am?" said Lito.

"How do you feel when you dance?" Dad asked.

Lito thought for a moment. "Happy," he said. "I'm Filipino, and I dance. I'm showing people who I am and how great Filipino dances are."

"And that's all that matters," his dad said. "Keep dancing, Lito. I'm proud of you."

Chapter 3
FESTIVAL TIME

It was the day of the school festival.
The show was about to start. Lito peeked
from backstage.

"Those boys are here," he told Nenita.

"Don't be scared, Lito," Nenita said. "Show them who you are!"

The boys laughed as Lito stepped onstage with Nenita.

The music started. The two kids with the poles tapped them on the floor twice. Then they clapped the poles together.

Tap, tap, clap! Tap, tap, clap!

Lito and Nenita began hopping between the moving poles. Lito tucked his arms behind him. Nenita held the sides of her skirt. The pair turned to the right and to the left. They spun around and around. They didn't miss a step.

Next, Lito took his sister's hand. Together, they skipped and twirled between the poles.

Nenita then stepped aside and left Lito on his own. The music played a little faster, and the poles moved faster too.

Tap, tap, clap! Tap, tap, clap!

Lito's knees pumped up and down. He was dancing well. When the music sped up again, the poles really tapped and clapped!

Tap, tap, clap! Tap, tap, clap!

Lito's toes brushed up against a pole.

He wobbled, but he didn't fall.

"Go, Lito!" Nenita shouted.

Lito breathed hard. His legs hurt. But he danced on. It looked like his feet weren't even touching the floor.

The boys in the front row stared, their mouths open. They were not laughing anymore. They were amazed!

Lito took Nenita's hand. They jumped and twirled between the bamboo poles again.

When the music stopped, Lito and
Nenita stopped. They raised their arms
high into the air.

The crowd cheered. Lito and Nenita's
parents stood up and yelled. The boys
in front clapped. One even gave a
thumbs-up. Lito and Nenita bowed.

"Now, aren't you glad you kept dancing?" Nenita asked.

"I sure am!" Lito said with a big smile.

JUMPING OVER THORNS

This is a Filipino game called Luksong tinik (LOOK-song TEE-neek), or Jumping Over Thorns. Tinikling dancers must be quick and light on their feet. Practice your jumping skills with this fun game. The goal is to jump over the other team's feet and hands (the "thorns") without touching them.

What You Need:
- at least three friends
- space to run and jump

What You Do:
1. Split into two teams, Team A and Team B.
2. Two players from Team A are the base. They sit on the ground with the bottoms of their feet touching.
3. Players on Team B take turns jumping over the feet.
4. Once everyone on Team B has jumped, the base players add more "thorns." One base puts a right hand on top of their feet (palm out with the little finger touching a foot). The other base stacks his/her right hand on top of the first hand. Palms should face out and the hands should be stacked little finger to thumb.
5. Team B takes turns jumping again. If everyone on Team B clears the thorns, the base players add another hand on top of the first one.
6. Repeat steps 4 and 5 until someone on Team B touches the thorns. Then the teams switch places and start again.

REPLAY IT

Take another look at this illustration. How do you think Lito felt as he walked onto the stage? How would you feel if you were in that same position?

Now pretend you are Lito. Write a letter to your grandparents telling them all about your dance at the festival.

ABOUT THE AUTHOR

Cristina Oxtra is a Filipino American author. She earned an MFA in creative writing for children and young adults at Hamline University. She is a recipient of the Loft Literary Center's 2019-2020 Mirrors & Windows Fellowship for indigenous writers and writers of color. Her books include *Stephen Hawking: Get to Know the Man Behind the Theory, Stan Lee: Get to Know the Comics Creator, Tae Kwon Do Test, Tara and the Towering Wave: An Indian Ocean Tsunami Survival Story,* and a Manga graphic novel titled *Red Riding Hood*.

ABOUT
THE ILLUSTRATOR

Seb Burnett is an illustrator and game developer living in Bristol, United Kingdom. When not drawing he loves going on long walks through the woods and hunting for monsters. He hasn't found any yet.